Meg and Merlin

Showing Off

Meg and Merlin

Showing Off

TANYA LANDMAN

Illustrated by
Sònia Albert

Barrington Stoke

To Buz

First published in 2022 in Great Britain by
Barrington Stoke Ltd
18 Walker Street, Edinburgh, EH3 7LP

www.barringtonstoke.co.uk

Text © 2022 Tanya Landman
Illustrations © 2022 Sònia Albert

A CIP catalogue record for this book is available
from the British Library upon request

ISBN: 978-1-80090-093-6

Printed by Hussar Books, Poland

CONTENTS

CHAPTER 1

Daydreaming

Meg was helping Dad with the weekly shop. They'd packed everything into bags at the checkout and were just going back to the car when Meg spotted a poster pinned to the noticeboard.

Fun for all the family!!
The Woodford Show
Sunday, 1 June. Save the date!!

Around the edges of the poster were photos
of all the things that would be at the show.
A bouncy castle. Burger and ice-cream

vans. A Punch and Judy show. Goats. Sheep.
Cows. Horses.

Horses!

Meg stopped dead.

Every year, if they could afford it, Meg's
parents took her to the County Show near
where her grandma lived. It was a big event,
crammed with thousands of people and
animals, vintage cars and motorbikes and
tractors.

Meg loved watching the horses best. They
came in all shapes and sizes, from shaggy
Shetland ponies to enormous Shire horses who
had their manes and tails plaited and their
coats brushed until they gleamed like polished
wood. Whatever their size, the horses stood in
the show ring with their heads held high until

the judge announced which of them was the
most handsome.

And then there was the Showjumping.
She'd always daydreamed about taking part –
riding a brilliant pony over big jumps with
awesome skill, getting a clear round in record
time, winning a dozen rosettes. But until now,
daydreams were all that Meg had.

Meg had always longed for a pony. She
knew that Mum and Dad couldn't afford to buy
her one and so Meg didn't make a fuss. But
she had wanted a pony of her own so badly
that it hurt.

And then, on the morning of her tenth
birthday, all her wishes came true. Almost.
Meg had looked out of her bedroom window
and seen a pony standing in the front garden.

4

The pony was called Merlin, but he wasn't the surprise present Meg had wished for. He belonged to a woman called Mrs Hill and her daughter Isobel.

Isobel was away at university and Merlin had got bored without her to ride him. So he'd escaped from his field and found his way to Meg's house. Meg had ridden him back to where he belonged. And Mrs Hill was so grateful that she said Meg could ride Merlin as often as she liked.

What Meg would have liked was to put up a tent in Merlin's field and live there. But living in a field with a pony wasn't allowed. Things like school and homework got in the way. And helping with the shopping.

Meg went on looking at the Woodford Show poster, her mind whizzing. She wouldn't ever be able to take Merlin to the big County Show –

it was too far away to ride to and they didn't have a horsebox. And really, she thought, she'd be scared to death of competing in something as grand as that.

But the Woodford Show looked as if it might be much smaller. More friendly.

"Where's Woodford?" asked Meg.

"It's the other side of Hunts Cross," Dad replied.

"Close enough to ride to?" said Meg.

Dad nodded. "I reckon it is. Fancy yourself in the ring, do you?" He smiled. "You must ask Mrs Hill. But I can't see her saying no, can you? Merlin will love it."

U

Daydreaming

Meg spent ages looking at the Woodford Show programme. The competitions were called classes and there were all kinds of different ones, from Showing to Showjumping, from Handy Pony to Mounted Games. There was even a Fancy Dress. Which should she enter?

Meg thought long and hard but in the end decided she didn't want to do any of the Showing classes. Merlin was handsome enough to win, she knew that. But she'd seen those classes at the County Show and knew that the riders had to look as perfect as their horses.

Meg's riding gear came from charity shops. Her tweed hacking jacket was baggy and had a patch on one elbow. Her jodhpurs were worn thin at the knees. They were fine for every day but not for a Show class.

In any case, Meg thought, winning a rosette just for having a beautiful pony and wearing the right clothes was silly. If she and Merlin won anything it would be because the pair of them had earned it.

She'd try the Handy Pony. It was a test of how well a pony and rider could do various tasks. No one took it too seriously.

She really wanted to put herself down for the Showjumping. Sometimes if they were out in the woods, she and Merlin came across a fallen tree or a stream that he'd jump easily. But she'd never ridden him over proper, painted show jumps and she didn't think she felt brave enough to try for the first time in public. Not on her own.

There was a Pairs class that looked like fun, but she didn't have any friends who had their own horses. She'd just do the Handy Pony then. That would be enough for her first show.

Meg filled in the entry form in her best handwriting and posted it off. Now all she had to do was wait for the big day to arrive.

CHAPTER 2

The Big Day Dawns

Sunday, 1 June. 6.30 a.m. Show time!

Meg's eyes snapped open and she was wide awake at once. Meg was looking forward to the show, but she was a little scared too.

Mum gave Meg a lift over to Merlin's field. Meg had taken his tack home the night before and given it a really good clean. Now she had to do the same to Merlin. She wanted him looking his best for the big day.

When they got to the field, Meg stared at Merlin, horrified. It had rained in the night and he was having a really good roll in the fresh mud.

As Meg climbed out of the car she could see him lying down, neck stretched out, swishing his head from one side to the other, rubbing his

face in the mud, working it into his cheeks as if it was a face pack.

When he saw Meg, he got to his feet and whinnied a happy greeting at her.

"There you are at last!" he seemed to be saying. "Come and join me! This stuff's great."

"Oh my word!" Mum laughed. "What a sight. You're going to have a terrible time getting him clean."

"Better get started then," said Meg.

"We'll see you at the show later, all right?" said Mum. "We'll wait for you at the ringside."

Mum drove away, leaving Meg to tackle the muddiest pony that she had ever seen.

U

When it was time to set off for the show, Merlin was clean from head to hoof, but Meg was filthy. Luckily, she had worn old clothes to get Merlin ready and she'd kept her jodhpurs and jacket in a bag. She got changed in the shelter in Merlin's field before they left. But she wished she'd had time for a shower!

Meg also wished she'd been able to plait Merlin's mane. She had started to, but his mane was so long and thick the plaits looked

like sausages. And the elastic bands kept pinging off. When one hit her in the eye, Meg gave up. If they didn't set off now, they'd never get to the show on time.

Merlin somehow knew that today was special.

"Where are we going? What are we doing? What's going on?" he seemed to ask as he stepped out in a brisk, eager walk.

As they got closer to the showground Meg wasn't sure if she was really, really excited or if she was going to be sick. Something seemed to be doing a dance inside her tummy.

Meg had what Grandma always called the collywobbles.

Merlin always paid such close attention to Meg when they were out it felt like he could read her thoughts. He did what she asked almost before she'd done anything. But when they arrived at the Woodford Show, Merlin's head was full of thoughts of his own. He could hear and smell and see other horses. And they all seemed to have an awful lot to say to each other.

Merlin whinnied. A long, high yell of excitement. It was answered by a horse somewhere across the showground, so Merlin did it again. And again.

Meg had a hard time holding him back. Merlin's walk was so bouncy he might have had springs on his hooves, not horseshoes. Meg felt as if she was perched on an unexploded bomb that might go off at any second.

She needed to keep him steady, Meg told herself. She took deep breaths, relaxed her shoulders and tried to pretend it was just the

two of them out for a nice little ride in the country. Slowly, Merlin started to respond. They could do this, she thought. This was going to be fun. Really. It was.

Meg had planned to arrive early and give Merlin time to settle down before the Handy Pony class got started. But it had taken so long to get him clean that the class was already being called over the loudspeaker.

She steered Merlin through the crowds to the smallest of the ground's three show rings. They joined the group of riders who were waiting to compete. Mum and Dad were at the ringside and Meg gave them a smile and a cheerful wave.

But then she saw Sam Houseman and Meg started to feel sick all over again.

CHAPTER 3

Little Miss Perfect

Sam Houseman was in the year above Meg at school. Meg had never spoken to her, but she knew her name. Everybody did. Sam Houseman was "Little Miss Perfect". Pretty and clever, the teachers loved her. But Sam seemed to think she was better than all the other kids in the school. Everyone said she was really stuck-up.

And now here was Sam, sitting on a pony whose coat gleamed like a fresh conker. The pony was almost as beautiful as Merlin and was much better groomed. Sam's pony had its black mane tied into perfect, tight little plaits. These were the ones that Meg had been trying to do with Merlin, and the top of its tail was plaited too.

Sam and her pony looked as if they'd ridden right out of the pages of a glossy magazine. And they seemed to have been sprayed with some sort of invisible coating that kept off things like mud. Last night's rain had churned up the ground and everyone else's ponies had spatters of dirt on their legs and bellies. But not Sam's.

Perhaps Sam noticed Meg staring at her. Because suddenly she turned her head and her eyes met Meg's. Sam frowned and she gave Meg a sort of nod without saying anything. But then she looked Meg over more slowly. Sam stared at the jodhpurs with the worn knees. The too-big jacket with the patch on the elbow. And her lips pinched together as if she was trying not to smile.

Meg felt hot and awkward. She shifted in her saddle. And then she had a terrible thought. Where had her jodhpurs and hacking jacket come from? Who had given them to

the charity shop? Meg's tummy flipped over. Was she wearing Sam Houseman's old riding clothes?

Meg had felt so confident about the Handy Pony class. Merlin and she had come across all sorts of scary things when they were out riding. Black bin bags that flapped in the wind, bits of rope in puddles that Merlin thought were water snakes about to attack.

Meg knew that she could get him past anything if she was calm and confident. The trouble was that now she'd seen Sam, Meg wasn't feeling calm or confident at all.

Deep breaths. Deep breaths, Meg told herself.

Sam was first into the ring. The course was a set of tests. First, you had to ride your pony in and out along a line of upright poles

which had bags and ribbons pinned on top
of them.

Next you had to ride under a washing line
with clothes pegged to it that were flapping
in the wind. Then across a piece of tarpaulin
and through a shallow pond that was full of
rubber ducks.

After that, you had to trot to a horsebox. Dismount. Lead your pony up the ramp and out of the side door. Remount and trot in a circle around a person who was twirling an umbrella. Last, canter back across the ring, over the small brushwood jump and across the finish line.

Meg watched closely while Sam completed an almost perfect round. Her pony shot backwards when he was asked to go under the washing line, but that was all. A smartly dressed woman – Sam's mother? – barked from the ringside, "Get him moving, Sammy! Legs! Legs!"

Sam did as she was told and the pony suddenly put its head down and charged like a bull under the washing line, huffing and puffing with relief when it reached the other side.

Sam would get high scores for that round, Meg thought.

The next rider wasn't so lucky. Her pony thought that everything in the ring was terrifying. It leapt backwards, forwards and from side to side and then stopped dead. In the end, the rider gave up.

There were four more after that who did well but not as well as Sam. Then it was Meg's turn.

Keep calm and Merlin will be calm, Meg told herself. But her heart was hammering and her hands were clammy on the reins.

Mum and Dad were watching. Sam was watching. It felt like the whole world was watching.

Meg breathed in. Counted to three. Breathed out. She could do this. Merlin could do this. They could do this together. She and Merlin would show stuck-up Sam Houseman and her perfect pony!

It began well.

"Are we going in and out of the poles?" Merlin seemed to say. "I'm good at this!"

And then, "Under the flappy things on the line? If you say so. Don't like the crackly cloth thing on the ground. Let's get over it quickly, shall we? Can I jump across the pond? No? Walk through? Boring! All right. Those ducks are very odd. In and out of the big box? All right."

But then they came to the person twirling the umbrella and Merlin stopped still and went stiff as if he wanted to bolt away.

"What's that thing? I don't like it," he was saying. "Can we run?"

Meg could feel everyone looking at her. Mum and Dad willing her on. Sam wanting her to fail.

"It's OK," said Meg. "Nothing to worry about. It's only an umbrella."

She thought positive thoughts. She carried on breathing deeply and felt Merlin relax a little. But suddenly a gust of wind filled the umbrella and flipped it inside out with a loud SNAP!

Meg jumped. And after that Merlin knew that he was right. The umbrella *was* scary.

"Run!" he thought, wheeling around so suddenly that Meg lost both her stirrups. Merlin went one way. Meg went the other. She landed in the mud with a splat!

Merlin was so surprised that Meg had fallen off that he stopped dead. He turned, looked down at her and blew a puff of warm breath into Meg's face.

"Are you all right?" Merlin was asking. "What are you doing in the mud? Are you going to have a good roll?"

Meg got slowly to her feet. She wasn't hurt. She just felt stupid.

"Straight back on, there's a good girl," shouted the judge.

Meg remounted and cantered Merlin over the jump and across the finish line. She'd got round the course at least. But falling off like that? There was no chance of a rosette now.

"That was terribly bad luck," the judge said with a kind smile. "You'd been doing so well up until then. Next time you'll fly through."

But Meg didn't think there would be a next time. Sam Houseman had seen Meg landing in the mud. Everyone at school would be talking about it tomorrow and having a good laugh.

Suddenly Meg knew that she didn't belong here at the show with all these rich horsey people.

She wanted to go home.

CHAPTER 4

A Perfect Pair?

After the Handy Pony class had finished and Sam Houseman had been given her red rosette, Meg left Mum and Dad holding Merlin's reins and headed for the toilets. There wasn't any point staying, she thought. After she'd had a wee, she'd start the ride back to Merlin's field.

When Meg came out of the Portaloo, she ran smack bang into Sam.

"I'm sorry, I'm sorry!" gabbled Sam, her hands up. But when she saw who she'd crashed into, she turned bright red.

The two girls stared at each other for a second or two.

"Are you all right?" Sam blurted suddenly. "That was a nasty fall." Her voice was too loud, as if she was worried or scared.

Meg looked at her surprised and Sam blushed even more.

This is odd, thought Meg. Sam seemed nervous. But that couldn't be right. Could it?

"I'm fine," said Meg. "No bones broken."

Another silence.

Then Sam said, "That's good. You were really unlucky with that umbrella ..." It

sounded as if Sam was making a real effort
to talk to Meg. As if she was trying hard but
didn't know what to say next. Everyone said
Sam was stuck-up. But perhaps she was just
shy?

Maybe Meg should make an effort too? But
what could they talk about? They only had one
thing in common ...

"You've got a lovely pony," said Meg.
"What's his name?"

"Alfred," said Sam, and at last she smiled
at Meg.

"His mane looks great plaited like that.
I tried to do that to Merlin this morning, but
his plaits just looked like sausages."

Sam laughed. Suddenly both the girls relaxed. "My mum did it," said Sam with a shrug. "She really likes the Show classes."

"Don't you?" Meg asked. She remembered the woman who'd shouted "Legs! Legs!" at Sam during the Handy Pony. She seemed sort of pushy.

"They're OK, I suppose," said Sam. "But it's just a beauty contest, isn't it? I like the Handy Pony better. And the Showjumping."

"Have you entered?"

"No ..." Sam blushed again. "I'm not really brave enough!"

There was a pause. The girls both seemed to be thinking the same thing.

Meg looked up at the sky, "They do a Pairs class."

"Yes, I know," said Sam, staring at the trees. "And you can enter on the day."

Another pause. "Do you think we ...?" Meg didn't finish her question.

Sam grinned. "I will if you will."

CHAPTER 5

Flying!

Meg and Sam put their names down for the Beginner Pairs Jumping. It wasn't starting for an hour, so they rode around the showground together first, laughing and chatting about ponies as if they'd been friends for years. Merlin and Alfred seemed to get on as well as the girls did.

And then it was time for the Showjumping to begin.

The course was like a figure of eight with ten jumps. Everyone who was taking part had to walk it first so that they remembered each bit. You had to do the jumps in the right order.

Suppose I forget? thought Meg. *What if I take a wrong turn? Or fall off again? And even if I don't, even if I get a clear round – what if I'm too slow? They take points off for that.*

Sam seemed to be as worried as Meg.

"What if I get the jumps in the wrong order?" she said in a whisper.

"It'll be fine," said Meg. "It's only a bit of fun." She knew she sounded confident, but inside she felt sick with nerves.

They watched the first pair – a boy and a girl who looked so alike they had to be brother and sister.

The girl went first, sailing clear over everything and cantering back to her brother. She slapped his hand – the signal that it was his turn – and he was off. But maybe his pony was more skittish or he wasn't such a good rider, because his pony ran out at the fourth fence and didn't jump it. The boy tried again

and again, but each time his pony refused to go over the jump.

And so the pair were eliminated. The boy looked as if he was trying not to cry, but his sister said cheerfully, "Never mind, Tom! Let's go get an ice cream."

It was Meg and Sam's turn.

Sam was looking nervous, so Meg went first. Merlin was longing to get going and when the bell rang, giving the signal for them to start, he took off like a rocket before Meg had nudged his sides with her heels. He flew over the first fence.

"Where next?" he seemed to ask.

Meg fixed her eyes on the second fence and Merlin read her thoughts.

"That one?" he said. "Got it!"

He cantered towards it, taking the turn much tighter than Meg would have dared, and cleared it easily. The third and fourth fences were close together and in a straight line ahead. Meg kept her eyes fixed on them and Merlin followed her signal.

Meg hadn't done any Showjumping with Merlin, but his owner Isobel Hill clearly had. The pony was absolutely loving it.

It was as if he was telling Meg, "I've been dying to do this for ages! What took you so long?"

Meg had had a few jumping lessons at the riding stables before she'd met Merlin, but she hadn't much enjoyed them. It had always been such an effort to get the riding-school ponies over the fences. Sometimes Meg had felt like getting off and leaping the jumps by herself to save them the effort.

But with Merlin everything was different. To him, jumping was the most exciting thing on earth. He'd missed this. And now he was flying round and enjoying every second.

He took the fifth and the sixth fences happily, but at the seventh a child in the watching crowd let their balloon go by mistake. The balloon drifted across the show ring right in front of Meg and Merlin. On a normal ride Merlin would have been spooked. But he was having so much fun, he didn't even notice.

Over the seventh fence, the eighth. The ninth. Almost there! Meg didn't relax even though they were so close to the end. They leapt the tenth and cantered over the finishing line, Meg slapping Sam's hand as she passed her.

"Done it," Meg said, giving the lightest squeeze of Merlin's reins and sitting deep in the saddle.

Merlin took a while to slow down.

"Can we do it again?" he seemed to be saying, trotting on the spot. "Can we? Can we?"

By the time Merlin had agreed to stand still, Sam and Alfred had reached the fourth fence.

They were going well, clearing the fifth and sixth easily, but Meg wasn't sure if they were as fast as she and Merlin had been.

Alfred jumped the seventh with no problem, but when they came to the eighth he put in a funny little extra step before it, which threw Sam off balance. When he took off, Sam got left behind. Instead of leaning low over his neck as Alfred jumped, she was flicked back and the pair didn't land properly on the other side.

From the ringside Sam's mother gave an angry yell that Meg heard right across the ring.

"Oh, Sammy!"

And after that, Sam couldn't get it all back together. Alfred just about cleared the ninth fence, but at the tenth and last jump his hoof caught the pole, which rattled and then fell.

U

"Sorry," said Sam for the thousandth time when it was all over. "You were so fast! We'd have won if I'd jumped a clear round."

The two girls were riding home from the show together. It turned out that Alfred's stable was only a mile from Merlin's field. They were going to meet up next weekend and have a ride in the woods together.

"Don't be sorry," said Meg. And she really meant it. "I'd never have even entered without you. It was brilliant."

What a day it had been, Meg thought when she turned Merlin out into his field. He had a good long roll and was soon as caked with mud as he had been that morning. It seemed like a long time ago now. Back then Meg had dreamed of coming home with a rosette. But now she didn't care about that.

She and Merlin had won something far better.

Friends.

Find out how Meg and Merlin met in ...

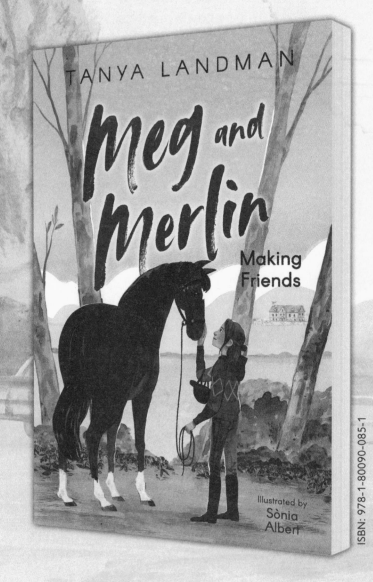

TANYA LANDMAN

Meg and Merlin

Making Friends

Illustrated by
Sònia Albert

ISBN: 978-1-80090-085-1

Then follow them on their
next adventure in ...

Meg and Merlin

Running Away

COMING SOON!

ISBN: 978-1-80090-173-5

Our books are tested
for children and young people by
children and young people.

Thanks to everyone who consulted on
a manuscript for their time and effort in
helping us to make our books better
for our readers.